# FOOTBALL
## FOUL PLAY

## BY JAKE MADDOX

text by
Eric Stevens

STONE ARCH BOOKS
a capstone imprint

Published by Stone Arch Books, an imprint of Capstone.
1710 Roe Crest Drive
North Mankato, Minnesota 56003
capstonepub.com

Library of Congress Cataloging-in-Publication Data
Names: Maddox, Jake, author. | Stevens, Eric, 1974– author.
Title: Football foul play / Jake Maddox ; text by Eric Stevens.
Description: North Mankato, Minnesota : Stone Arch Books, [2022] | Series: Jake Maddox JV mysteries | Audience: Ages 8–11. | Audience: Grades 4–6. | Summary: Everyone on the Bader Ginsburg Middle School Badgers is looking forward to the playoffs and a chance to win back the Supreme Bowl trophy from the Wellstone Middle School Warriors—but somebody has stolen the trophy, and evidence points to one of the Badgers, so teammates Kenny Hu and Romeo Russell set out to clear their friend and discover the truth.
Identifiers: LCCN 2021012665 (print) | LCCN 2021012666 (ebook) | ISBN 9781663920287 (paperback) | ISBN 9781663911155 (hardcover) | ISBN 9781663911124 (ebook pdf)
Subjects: LCSH: Football stories. | Theft—Juvenile fiction. | Friendship—Juvenile fiction. | Detective and mystery stories. | CYAC: Mystery and detective stories. | Football—Fiction. | Stealing—Fiction. | Friendship—Fiction. | LCGFT: Detective and mystery fiction. | Sports fiction.
Classification: LCC PZ7.M25643 Fn 2021 (print) | LCC PZ7.M25643 (ebook) | DDC 813.6 [Fic]—dc23
LC record available at https://lccn.loc.gov/2021012665
LC ebook record available at https://lccn.loc.gov/2021012666

Editorial Credits
Editor: Amber Ross; Designer: Tracy Davies; Media Researcher: Jo Miller; Production Specialist: Katy LaVigne

Image Credits: Shutterstock/JoeSAPhotos, cover

# TABLE OF CONTENTS

# CHAPTER 1

# JUST THE BEGINNING

Kenny Hu sprinted up the field toward the end zone. The damp turf sent a spray from his feet. His socks were soaked. The fine rain ran down his face shield.

Kenny easily outran his defender. It was late in the game, and his team, the Bader Ginsburg Middle School Badgers, were already ahead by thirteen points.

They would clinch a spot in the postseason for sure. But Kenny wasn't just interested in winning.

He also wanted to set his personal best for scoring in a single game.

At the end zone, he cut to the left. His defender, already five steps behind, slid on the wet grass. At this moment, his teammate Jasper Kane, the quarterback, would be launching a pass to him.

Kenny glanced over his shoulder and found the ball spiraling toward him through the mist.

He smiled as he put out his hands and caught the ball for another six points. That gave him thirty points, or five touchdowns, on the day.

As the game ended, Jasper and Kenny's best friend, Romeo Russell, ran through the rain to the end zone. The three of them—as quarterback, wide receiver, and center lineman—made a great offensive trio.

"I wasn't sure you'd grab that one in this rain," Jasper said, patting Kenny's helmet.

Kenny gave him a little shove, smiling. "And I wasn't sure you'd throw a decent pass with wet hands," he said.

"I thought you'd both slip on the grass and end up in the mud," Romeo said, laughing.

Back in the locker room, Coach Zevrin clapped for the boys as they celebrated. "Great game, everyone," he said. "The postseason begins next weekend."

"Which means we can finally get the Bowl back from Wellstone," Kenny said.

The other boys on the team hooted and cheered.

The Badgers lost the Supreme Bowl—the league championship game—to the Wellstone Middle School Warriors ten years ago.

Since then, the Warriors had won every single Bowl. The Badgers hadn't even made it to the postseason.

Until now.

"I knew this would be the squad to get us there," Coach Zevrin said, "finally."

The boys cheered again.

"This year, we'll win that trophy," Coach Zevrin said, "and hold on to it for *fifty* years."

"Yeah we will!" Kenny shouted.

The others laughed and cheered.

"And that journey begins next weekend," Coach Zevrin said, trying to get the team to settle down a bit. "So while our sights are set on Wellstone, we first have to get past the Lincoln Lakers."

"Piece of cake," said Romeo.

He and Kenny high-fived.

"All right, go celebrate," the coach said, "and I'll see you Monday for practice. Here's where it gets real."

# CHAPTER 2

# THE QUARTERFINALS

The first week of the postseason, the Badgers faced the Lakers from Lincoln Middle School. The Lakers didn't have a record as strong as the Warriors. It wasn't as strong as the Badgers, either, for that matter.

But it wouldn't be a walk in the park.

The Lakers won the coin toss and chose to receive. The Badgers kicker, a seventh grader named Benny Haas, took the field with the rest of the special team.

Benny was a star soccer player. He hadn't even wanted to play football. But Kenny, Jasper, and Romeo convinced him. They knew he'd be a great kicker, and they promised he'd never get hurt.

That's why Romeo, normally the center, volunteered to join the special team too: to protect Benny.

The team lined up. Benny raised his right hand and jogged to the ball. He drew back his leg and, with perfect soccer form, slammed the football.

It soared above the field as the teams charged toward each other, their eyes on the ball.

The ball came down just past the fifty-yard line. The Lakers kick returner—a talented running back Kenny recognized from their game during the regular season—caught the ball. He took off up the sideline.

Romeo was pretty fast for a big guy. He cut the runner off before the forty-five and easily brought him down.

The Lakers offense took the field. The Badgers defense hustled out to face them.

"Not an inch, boys," Kenny said, leading the cheer for the defense.

The Lakers ran three times, but the Badgers defense was as stubborn as their namesake. The Lakers didn't pick up a single yard. They were forced to punt.

Romeo and Kenny took the field as part of the punt-return team.

The Lakers lined up. For a moment, Romeo thought they might fake the kick. At the snap, he slammed into the offensive line as the Lakers kicker drew back and punted.

Kenny caught the punt near the fifteen-yard line. He took off like a shot, dodging to his right and spinning toward the sideline, avoiding three charging Lakers.

"Go, Kenny!" Jasper yelled from the sideline.

Most of the Lakers offensive line barreled down the sideline toward Kenny. He turned diagonally toward the center of the field and sprinted, forcing the offensive line to cut across too.

Romeo charged with him. He wasn't as fast as Kenny, but he was fast enough to meet a couple of the Lakers tacklers. He grunted as he felt the impact of the two linemen, but he slowed them down enough to let Kenny gain a few more yards.

The Lakers tacklers finally took Kenny down at the fifty. He hurried to the bench for a drink. Jasper jumped to his feet and gave Kenny's shoulder a pat.

"Nice run," he said.

Romeo joined them and grabbed a cup of water. He pushed up his helmet and drank it down.

"Let's not waste it now," he said, breathing heavily.

"That's right," Coach Zevrin said. "Get out there and turn that run into a conversion for us, Hu."

The offense took the field for the Badgers. In the huddle, Jasper called for a play-action pass.

Kenny lined up at the right end of the offensive line. Jasper took the snap. He faked a hand-off to the running back, Lucas Fump. Lucas pushed through the middle with Romeo clearing his path.

The defense fell for it. They crushed in on the center, trying to stop Lucas.

Meanwhile, Jasper rolled out to the left and threw a perfect spiral twenty yards to Kenny.

Kenny was wide open. He grabbed the ball and took off along the sideline, sprinting down the empty field and into the end zone for the game's first six points.

The Badgers excellent teamwork kept working for them over the rest of the game. When the clock ran out, the Badgers had their first win of the postseason, 24 to 10.

\* \* \*

Back in the locker room, after the game and after Coach Zevrin's brief speech, Kenny sat with Jasper and Romeo. They were all showered and changed.

The boys were tired after the game but also full of excited energy. They'd won the first game of the postseason, and they'd won decisively.

"The Bowl is as good as ours," Jasper said. He sat on a bench and leaned way back, resting his shoulders on a nearby locker.

"Don't get cocky," Kenny said.

"Yeah, that's Kenny's job," Romeo added. He covered a laugh.

Kenny gave him a playful punch in the arm.

"I'd better get going," Kenny said, sitting up. "My mom hates when I make her wait in the parking lot." He grabbed his bag of dirty football clothes.

Romeo got to his feet too and grabbed his laundry.

Jasper joined them.

"Forgetting something, stinky?" Romeo said to Jasper as the three boys walked out of the locker room. "Where's your uniform?"

"I'll wash it on Monday morning when I get to school," Jasper said. "There is a washing machine here, you know."

"Yeah, but it's not *free*," Kenny pointed out. "And the money on my card is for the snack bar in the cafeteria too."

Every kid in the school district carried a plastic card. They used it to pay for lunches, snack bar visits, library holds, and the laundry machines in the locker rooms.

He and Romeo high-fived. "Yeah, I'll save my card money for an extra drink and bag of chips, thanks," Romeo said, laughing.

When they reached the parking lot, Jasper waved at the blue minivan at the curb. "There's my mom," he said, breaking into a jog. "Good game, guys. See you Monday."

Both Kenny and Romeo lived very close to the school, and their parents had left after the game. With their laundry bags over their shoulders, Romeo and Kenny walked home.

# CHAPTER 3

# SMASHED!

On Monday morning, Kenny met up with Romeo for the walk to school.

"What's up, man?" Kenny said as he walked up to Romeo at the corner of Eighth and Dunlop. The boys bumped shoulders.

"I'm just fired up for Friday's game," Romeo said. "I don't know if I can wait five days to beat Mondale."

The Mondale Middle School Marauders were their next postseason opponent. The Badgers faced them twice during the regular season and won both games.

"You and Jasper and I have been playing great all year," Kenny said as the boys headed toward the school. "With the three of us against the Marauders, they don't have a chance of winning."

"Winning?" Romeo said, laughing. "They don't have a chance of stopping us even once. I predict you break some postseason scoring records this week."

"No doubt," Kenny said.

When the boys reached the school's main entrance, they found a crowd of people at the front doors—including Jasper, Principal Polaski, and Coach Zevrin. Jasper looked angry, and neither the principal nor the coach looked very happy either.

Kenny's stomach lurched. He knew right away this wasn't good news.

"What's going on?" Kenny asked.

A sixth grader near the edge of the crowd shrugged.

Kenny pushed through. He reached Jasper and grabbed his sleeve. "Hey, what's happening?" Kenny asked.

Jasper turned toward him, his eyes red and flashing with anger.

"Whoa," Kenny said, letting go of his arm. "You okay?"

"No, he's not," said Principal Polaski. She glared at Jasper, and then at Coach Zevrin.

"I didn't do it," Jasper said.

"Didn't do what?" Romeo asked as he pushed up next to Kenny.

The coach turned to Kenny and Romeo. "If either of you knows anything about this," he said, "it would be best to come forward now." He was stern and serious, not the good-hearted and jovial coach they were used to.

"It may seem like a harmless prank," Principal Polaski said, "but trespassing and property damage are *not* pranks. They're crimes."

Kenny looked at Romeo. Romeo looked back, eyes wide, and shrugged.

"Jasper," Kenny whispered, "what did you do?"

Jasper stomped his foot and turned away.

"Just a moment, young man," Principal Polaski said, making a move to stop him from going into the school.

Coach Zevrin put his hand up. "Give him a minute to cool off, okay?" he asked the principal.

She took a deep breath and nodded.

Jasper angrily pulled the door open and went into the school.

Principal Polaski took another deep breath. "All right, everyone," she said as she stepped toward the door. "Let's break it up and get to our advisory classrooms now."

"Coach?" Kenny said. "Wanna let us in on what's happening?"

"You two really don't know a thing about this?" Coach Zevrin asked. "I thought you three were inseparable."

"We usually are," Kenny said.

The coach sighed. "It seems someone snuck into Wellstone Middle School over the weekend," he said. "They smashed the display case and stole the Supreme Bowl trophy."

Kenny couldn't believe it. "What?!" he said.

"And according to a witness at Wellstone," the coach said, "it was Jasper Kane."

# CHAPTER 4

# GUILTY?

"I'm telling you," Jasper said through gritted teeth, "it wasn't me."

Kenny sat with his two best friends in the cafeteria. Only Romeo could eat, though.

"How could you eat at a time like this?" Jasper said. "I'm too angry to eat."

Romeo grunted and shook his head. "Anger just makes me hungry," he said.

"And I'm too confused to eat," Kenny said.

Romeo nodded as he spooned another bite of turkey stew into his mouth. "Yeah, confusion too," he said. "Makes me hungrier."

"Is there anything that doesn't make you hungry?" Kenny asked.

Romeo thought for a second. "My mom's olive fish loaf," he joked.

"Could you two be serious for like five seconds?" Jasper said. He picked up his tray and slammed it back down, earning some looks from the students nearby and withering glares from the on-duty teachers.

"Sorry," Kenny said.

"Yeah, sorry," Romeo added. He put down his spoon.

The three friends sat in silence for a few moments, none of them eating. Finally, Kenny spoke.

"Look, you didn't do it, right?" he asked.

Jasper squinted at him. "No, I didn't do it," he said.

"Fine, then eventually they'll figure that out, and you won't get in trouble," Kenny said.

"Right," Romeo said. "The truth has a way of coming out."

"Maybe," Jasper said.

Kenny got an idea. "Oh!" he said. "You need an alibi. What did you do this weekend? You know, like when the crime was committed?"

Jasper thought for a moment. "Not much," he admitted. "I played some computer games, did some homework. I saw you guys in Delta Strike Co-op on Saturday, remember?"

Kenny and his friends had played an online game together Saturday afternoon.

"Is that when the Bowl was stolen?" Romeo asked. "That would make this pretty easy!"

"No," Jasper said, his head hanging. "Polaski said someone saw me there on *Sunday* afternoon."

"What'd you do then?" Kenny asked, still hopeful.

"Nothing," Jasper said, shaking his head. "I think I was sleeping."

He leaned back in his chair. "Look," he said, "I appreciate what you guys are doing, really. But it's not gonna help. I'll probably get kicked off the team, and my football career will be over before I even get to high school. Just my luck."

He stood up, grabbed his tray, and hurried off. He tossed his tray into the bus bin and left the cafeteria.

"I'd hate to be in his shoes right now," Romeo said.

Kenny nodded. He couldn't even imagine what it would be like.

Quickly, he and Romeo finished their lunches and hurried after Jasper, probably already halfway to the math class they all shared.

To Kenny's surprise, though, Jasper was just outside the cafeteria.

"I'm afraid I have no choice, Jasper," Principal Polaski said. "You'll have to leave school grounds at once, and I'll have a meeting with you *and* your parents as soon as we can set it up."

She put a hand on his shoulder. "I'm extremely disappointed," she said. "Go get your stuff from your locker and meet me in my office in five minutes," she added before letting go and walking off.

"What was that all about?" Kenny asked.

"Just like I was saying," Jasper said. He wouldn't look Kenny in the eye. "They already think I'm guilty."

"But that's not fair!" Kenny protested.

Jasper shrugged. "They say they have me on video at Wellstone," he said, "smashing the glass and taking the Bowl."

Kenny's skin went cold. "Then it *was* you," he said quietly.

"Sure, why not," Jasper said. "And now I'm suspended from school and probably can't play football anymore. *And* I'll probably have to pay for the broken trophy case too."

Kenny didn't say anything. He just stared at his friend. If they had him on video, didn't that mean the case was closed? He was guilty?

"See you guys," Jasper said, ". . . probably never. Good luck with the postseason."

And with that, he stomped off to get his stuff and go home—maybe for good.

# CHAPTER 5

# JUST A PRANK

In math, Jasper's desk sat empty. Everyone in class seemed to know what had happened. Even as Dr. Hayley went over how to find the length of the long side of a right triangle, she sometimes glanced at Jasper's desk with a disappointed look on her face.

Kenny shook his head. "This stinks," he whispered to Romeo, who sat at the next desk over. "I can't believe he did that."

"And without even telling us," Romeo said.

"What, you would have gone with him?" Kenny asked.

"Heck yeah," Romeo said. "A heist? That's the ultimate, man. And with my two best buds?"

"Who said I would have gone?" Kenny said.

"You would have," Romeo insisted.

Kenny sat quietly and listened to Dr. Hayley. She wasn't paying any attention to him and Romeo at the back of the class.

Slowly and carefully, keeping his eyes on the teacher, Kenny slipped his phone out of his bag. Keeping it out of sight, he typed a text to Jasper: *Good prank though.*

A few seconds later, Jasper replied: *Leave me alone.*

*Maybe if you give the Bowl back and pay for the glass they'll let you play in the postseason*, Kenny offered.

Kenny waited, staring at his phone. He stared some more. No response.

"Come on, Jasper," Kenny hissed at the phone. "Reply already."

"Ahem."

Kenny looked up. Dr. Hayley stood at his desk and glared at him through the slim-lensed glasses at the tip of her nose.

"What do we say about phones in class, Mister Hu?" Dr. Hayley asked.

"Sorry," Kenny said. He tried to slip his phone back into his bag.

"Ah-ah," Dr. Hayley said. "I'll give it back to you after class." She put out her hand, palm up.

Kenny handed over the phone.

"Thank you," Dr. Hayley said as she walked back to the front of the classroom. "Now, Mister Hu, please come up to the whiteboard and solve for the length of the missing side using the Pythagorean theorem."

Romeo stifled a laugh—not very well—and Kenny grunted at him as he got up and made his way to the front of the room.

\* \* \*

When math class was over, Kenny went to Dr. Hayley's desk.

"Yes?" she said.

"My phone?" Kenny said.

"What about it?" Dr. Hayley asked, as if she'd forgotten all about it.

"Can I have it back?" Kenny asked. "Please?"

Dr. Hayley sighed. "This stays in your locker during classes from now on, right?" she said.

"Yes, I know," Kenny said. "I'm sorry. There's kind of a crisis going on and—"

"Save the drama for your mama," Dr. Hayley said, handing back the phone. "I don't want it in my class."

Kenny hurried after Romeo as he turned on his phone and checked his texts. There were two from Jasper:

*I. Didn't. Do. It.*

And . . .

*If you and Romeo were my friends you'd believe me.*

Romeo was waiting outside the classroom. Kenny showed him the texts.

"I mean," Romeo said, "he's not wrong."

"I know," Kenny said. He texted back: *Sorry. How can we help?*

# CHAPTER 6

# SECOND STRING

After last period, Kenny met up with Romeo outside the locker room. "This will be weird," Kenny said. "Practice without our quarterback."

"I guess Lucio will play," Romeo said.

Lucio Paoli was the second-string quarterback and a seventh grader.

"Says who?" Jasper said, appearing from around the corner.

"What are you doing here?" Kenny asked.

Jasper shrugged. "Principal Polaski didn't say I couldn't be on the team anymore," he replied. "So I figure it's up to Coach Zevrin."

Kenny glanced at Romeo. Romeo looked back with his eyes wide.

The three boys went into the locker room. Coach Zevrin was there, and so was Lucio, already in his practice uniform.

Coach Zevrin's easy smile fell away at once. "I didn't think I'd see you again today, Jasper," he said.

"Why not?" Jasper asked. He didn't even try to hide his anger and frustration. "I'm still on the team, aren't I?"

Coach Zevrin sighed. "Officially, yes," he admitted. "But your suspension has already begun, which means you're not . . . *welcome* at practices."

Kenny watched Jasper's face as his jaw clenched. For a second, Kenny thought his friend might explode with rage. But instead, Jasper just turned away. He didn't even slam the locker room door as he left.

"Boys," the coach said, turning to Kenny and Romeo. "I'm going to lean on you a lot over the next couple of weeks to take Lucio under your wings."

"What do you mean?" Kenny asked.

"He hasn't had much game time this season," the coach said, "but he's about to start in some of the most important games of the year. I want you two to help him call plays, and help him pull off play-actions and bootlegs. Those fake-out moves take a lot of practice. Can I count on you?"

"Yeah, of course," Kenny said. The truth was, though, he was a little annoyed at Lucio. It wasn't his fault Jasper was suspended, obviously, but Kenny couldn't help holding it against Lucio anyway.

Kenny and Romeo went to their lockers to get changed. Jasper's locker was slightly open. Kenny could just see the sleeve of his friend's jersey through the open door. Romeo went to shut it.

"Wait a second," Kenny said. He opened the locker all the way. "Jasper's uniform is here."

"So?" Romeo said. He pulled his own uniform out of his bag. "He left it here on Friday, remember?"

"Yeah, but it's clean," Kenny said. "He got sacked three times in the game on Friday. There's no way his jersey and pants would be this clean if he didn't wash them."

"So he came in over the weekend and washed them," Romeo said. "He told us he'd use the machines here, and clearly he did."

"But he didn't tell us he came to school when we asked him what he did this weekend," Kenny said.

"Dude, that's kind of boring," Romeo said. "I don't tell you every time I do my laundry. He probably did it this morning then."

Kenny shook his head. "He couldn't have," he said as he pulled on his own jersey. "Polaski and Zevrin stopped him on the way in. He never had a chance to get to the locker room to start a wash."

"All right, that does sound weird, I guess," Romeo admitted. "But so what?"

"I think something fishy is going on," Kenny said. He slammed Jasper's locker.

Romeo shrugged. "Maybe you're on to something," he said. "But right now, we have to make sure Jasper's sub doesn't blow the postseason for us. So let's go show Lucio the ropes."

* * *

Out on the field, Kenny and Romeo ran some passing drills with Lucio at quarterback and Gil, a cornerback, defending.

"Hut one," Lucio said, "hut. Hut!"

Romeo snapped the ball. Lucio faded back, and Kenny took off down the field.

Ten yards out, he cut to his right, shook off Gil, and turned—but the pass came two yards behind him. He tried to grab it but missed.

"Sorry!" Lucio called out. "I just need to get warmed up."

Kenny shook his head and jogged back to the line.

"Let's try the same one again," Kenny said. "Don't forget the play-action. You gotta pretend Lucas is in motion; he's doing wind sprints."

"Okay, I know," Lucio said. He took the snap and turned as Kenny sprinted upfield.

Lucio faked to his invisible running back, and then he faded right.

Kenny cut to his right to shake off Gil.

He put up his hands as Lucio's pass shot toward him. This time it was a little too far out. Diving, he got his fingertips on the ball, but he couldn't grab it. He landed on his chest on the turf.

Gil helped him up. "Man, I miss Jasper," Gil said.

"Tell me about it," Kenny agreed. He brushed off his jersey.

"Sorry!" Lucio called again. "My arm's a little stiff. I'll get you this time."

* * *

Coach Zevrin set up his offensive line with red jerseys. They'd run play after play against the defensive line.

The red team huddled up. "All right, let's see a handoff to Lucas," Kenny said. "Play three. I'll run with him to block."

"Break!" the red team shouted as they left the huddle.

Lucio took the snap from Romeo. He drew back and turned to his right . . . as Lucas came around on his left. The handoff fell to the grass.

David Pahs, on the defense, dove through the line and scooped it up. Lucio tried to tackle him, but David knocked him down and sprinted to the end zone for a touchdown.

"Lucio," Kenny said, "play three. Lucas will roll past on your left."

"I know," Lucio said, thumping himself in the helmet. "I'm sorry. I just . . . I just need to run the plays a few more times. I'll get it."

Romeo stepped up next to Kenny. "He'd better," Romeo said, "or we don't have a chance of making it to the Supreme Bowl, never mind winning it."

# CHAPTER 7

# THE WITNESS

After practice, Kenny got changed and hurried into Coach Zevrin's office before he left for the night.

"I know, I know," the coach said before Kenny could even open his mouth. "Lucio isn't as good as Jasper. If we want a chance of winning the Supreme Bowl, Jasper should be playing."

"No, that's not what—" Kenny started.

Coach Zevrin cut him off. "But the fact is," the coach went on, "your friend tried to get his hands on the Bowl the easy way, the cheater's way. And now he's paying for it."

The coach sighed and sat in his chair. "We're *all* paying for it," he added under his breath.

"I actually wasn't going to complain about Lucio or about Jasper being suspended," Kenny said.

"Oh, you weren't?" Coach Zevrin asked. "Okay then. What's on your mind?"

"I was wondering," Kenny said, "can I see the video of the person stealing the Supreme Bowl?"

The coach looked surprised. "If I had it to show you, I would," he said. "But I did see the footage myself and it was Jasper."

"You saw his face?" Kenny asked.

"I saw the baseball cap he always wears," the coach said, "with the Bearcats team logo on it. And of course his jersey."

"Wait, what?" Kenny asked.

"His game jersey," the coach said. "Badgers number fourteen. That's Jasper, isn't it?"

They both knew it was. And they both knew that the football players liked to wear their game jerseys on off days, especially if they'd just won on Friday.

Kenny had worn his on Sunday, too.

"So I guess he did come in and get his jersey over the weekend," Kenny muttered to himself.

"What's that?" the coach asked.

"Oh, nothing," Kenny said. "Just trying to figure out when he could have come in to wash his jersey.

"Did anyone else see him?" Kenny asked. "Didn't you say there was a witness, too?"

"Right," Coach Zevrin said. "A bus maintenance guy at Wellstone named McAnnany. George, I think."

The coach grabbed his windbreaker and shoulder bag. "I have to get going, Mr. Hu," he said. "I'll see you tomorrow."

With that, the coach motioned for Kenny to leave.

"Okay, see you tomorrow, Coach," he said.

He hurried outside and caught up with Romeo on the sidewalk in front of the school. "Hey, wanna go on a field trip with me to Wellstone?" Kenny asked, jogging up to his friend.

"Right now?" Romeo asked.

"Yeah, why not?" Kenny said.

"Um, because Monday is pizza night at the Russell house?" he said. "And if I'm late, my two big sisters will *not* save me any pepperoni-and-hot-pepper slices."

"You'll be home by six," Kenny said.

"Promise?" Romeo asked.

"Six-thirty at the latest," Kenny hedged.

"Is this about Jasper somehow?" Romeo asked.

"Of course," Kenny said. "We need to do a little investigating, that's all."

"Fine," Romeo agreed. "If it's for Jasper, I'm in. But if there's only spinach-and-olive slices left, you owe me a pizza."

"Deal," Kenny said. "Let's go."

The boys hopped on the Fifth Street bus across town to Wellstone Middle School. They got off and found a man in green coveralls under the hood of a school bus.

"Excuse me," Kenny said. "Are you George McAnnany?"

The man came out from under the hood. He was an older guy, about Kenny's grandpa's age. He had grease on his right cheek, and his dark hair looked almost as oily as the pavement under the bus.

"That's me," he said, smiling. "Do I know you two?"

George seemed friendly enough.

"No," Kenny said. "We go to Bader Ginsburg."

"Way across town?" George asked. "What are you doing over here?"

Before Kenny answered, George's smile turned to a frown. He nodded gravely.

"Ah, the stolen Supreme Bowl," he said. "You know, I played for the Warriors back before this school was even called Wellstone. I played on the Bowl-winning team two years in a row!" George puffed out his chest. "We beat the Badgers back when it was called East Side Middle."

"Oh," Kenny said. He felt his face go red. Maybe George wasn't so friendly after all. "Well, my coach said it was you who saw the guy steal the trophy yesterday."

"Yup," George said. "Wasn't either of you. It was that quarterback you have over there—Jasper Kane."

"You know Jasper?" Romeo asked, surprised.

"I don't know him personally," George said. "But I do know he's number fourteen at our rival middle school, don't I? I follow school sports, don't I?"

"I guess you do," Kenny agreed.

"Darn right I do," George said. "And I saw that boy walk out of that front door with the Bowl under his arm, and he was wearing one of *your* team jerseys"—he gave Kenny a couple of pokes in the chest as he spoke—"with the number fourteen on the front and back.

"Now, I'm no detective," George continued, "but I can add two and two, and mister, where I come from, that makes four."

Kenny looked at Romeo, and Romeo shrugged. "I mean, it does make four," he agreed. "That's just math."

"Darn right," George said. "Your friend's smart. Now why don't you two get outta here before you get it in your mind to steal something else."

With that, he stuck his head back under the bus's hood. Together, Kenny and Romeo returned to the bus stop.

"Well, that was useless," Kenny said.

"Not really," Romeo argued. "We know two plus two is four now."

"We knew that already," Kenny said.

"*And*," Romeo went on, "we know that old George there has no idea what Jasper looks like. He only knows his jersey number."

"So?" Kenny asked.

"So," Romeo said, "anyone could have been wearing his jersey on Sunday afternoon. Maybe it wasn't Jasper after all."

# CHAPTER 8

# TOO CLOSE

Over the course of the week, Kenny and Romeo were busy. They went to school and to practice, and they tried to figure out who would want to frame Jasper, and how they did it.

All the while, they didn't hear a peep out of Jasper.

When Friday afternoon rolled around, they boarded the bus to Mondale Middle School to face the Marauders. Lucio sat with them in the back.

He had the coach's clipboard and went over the offensive playbook again and again.

"I think I've got it, you guys," Lucio said.

"I sure hope you do," Kenny said. "I don't wanna see Lucas charging the line from the backfield with nothing in his hands."

"Unless that's the play," Lucio said.

"You know what I mean," Kenny replied.

The bus squeaked to a stop at Mondale Middle, and the team climbed off. They hurried into the visitors' locker room.

"It's been a . . . weird week," Coach Zevrin said to the boys. Everyone had gathered around just before the game. "But we've practiced hard, and today we'll play hard."

The boys nodded, and Coach Zevrin continued. "If we work together as a team on offense, and with our defense at the strongest it's ever been," he told them, "we'll win out there today. Now let me get a Badgers."

The team shouted "Badgers!" together, and then got up and charged out of the locker room and onto the field.

The Marauders won the coin toss and chose to kick. Kenny caught the kickoff and ran it back to the Marauders forty-yard line.

He gave Romeo a high five when the center got to the line.

"Nice run," Romeo said.

"Let's see if we can do anything with it," he said. They both looked at Lucio as the seventh grader took the field.

Lucio set up behind Romeo for the snap.

Kenny stood a few feet back from the line on the left side, ready to run. It was play number five: a bootleg to a pass on the left sideline. Lucio should fake the handoff to Lucas, roll out to the left side, and find Kenny twenty yards out. If Kenny couldn't shake his defender, Lucio would be able to find another receiver straight out ten yards.

Lucio called for the snap. He turned to his right, faked the handoff, and rolled out to the left.

So far so good.

Kenny sprinted along the sideline, spun to lose his man, and turned around to find the ball spiraling toward him. It wasn't as good as a pass from Jasper, but he managed to get a hand on it and pull it in.

He got his footing and headed upfield, but the defender was back on him. He grabbed Kenny around the waist and pulled him down out of bounds.

It was a gain, and Kenny couldn't blame Lucio for a less-than-perfect pass. It was a pretty good pass, and they made the play for another first down.

He got up and jogged back to the huddle, clapping.

"Nice one, guys," he said as he joined the huddle. "Let's see if we can keep that magic going."

Lucio smiled, obviously pleased to have Kenny's approval.

But it wouldn't last. The team broke from the huddle and lined up for first down.

Kenny lined up on the left side, two steps back from the line.

He cut across the backfield, Romeo snapped the ball, and Lucio handed off to Lucas.

Lucas sprinted up the left side, with Kenny in front of him. He gained six yards and went down at the fourteen.

In the huddle, Kenny said, "Worst case, we're in field goal range, and we've got two downs to get the TD. Break!"

The Badgers lined up. Kenny rolled across the backfield and, on the snap, charged into the end zone.

Lucio launched a line drive pass . . .

. . . right into the defensive line.

A Marauders defender snatched the pass out of the air, leaped over the offensive line, and went down at his own twenty-yard line.

"I guess I spoke too soon," Kenny muttered to himself as he headed to the bench. "I sure wish Jasper were here."

* * *

The Badgers defense gave it their all. They held the Marauders to one TD and one field goal in the first three quarters. They even blocked the extra point kick. Unfortunately, the offense couldn't match that performance.

By the start of the fourth quarter, they'd only managed to put up two field goals for six points. As time wound down, they'd need a touchdown to win and stay alive in the postseason.

With only one minute left in the fourth quarter, the offense took the field.

"Lucio," Kenny said in the huddle, "you're nervous. I get it. But right now you need to find the zone. If we don't score on this push, it's over: the game, the season, and our chance at winning the Supreme Bowl."

"The *right* way," said Lucas, "not the cheater's way."

Kenny hadn't realized it, but a lot of the team was mad at Jasper for stealing the Bowl and making them all look like cheaters. Kenny still didn't believe Jasper did it, but it was getting harder and harder to think that way.

"Focus on the game, Fump," Romeo said with a little growl.

This burglary and vandalism were going to tear the team apart soon.

"Come on, break," Kenny said.

The offense lined up. Romeo snapped the ball. Lucio bootlegged and faded back. He passed to Kenny, but it flew too high and bounced at the Marauders thirty.

"At least it wasn't intercepted," Kenny muttered to himself. He jogged back to the huddle for second down.

"Let's try to focus out there, Lucio," Kenny said. "I was wide open. We need to make those plays."

"My arm's tired," Lucio said. "I've never had this much playtime in one game."

"Fine, then we run it," Kenny said. "Play five, to Lucas. Break!"

The offense lined up. Romeo snapped. Kenny rolled around behind the line and sprinted upfield.

Lucas took a dump pass just past the line of scrimmage. He spun from a tackler and ran up the right sideline for a gain of six yards.

Kenny jogged back to the huddle, clapping. "There we go," he said. "Third down, four to convert."

"We can tie it up and go into overtime with a field goal," Lucio said.

Kenny shook his head. "No ties," he ordered. "We're going to win it on this push."

"But—" Lucio protested.

"Fix your attitude, Lucio," Romeo said.

"Sorry," he said. "I just figured Benny has had a lot of rest, and maybe—"

"Play-action," Kenny said, interrupting him. "I'll go out ten yards, button hook."

"Another pass?" Lucio said.

"You can do this," Romeo said. "It's a short pass. Game's almost over. Dig deep."

Lucio nodded. "Okay," he said. "Break."

They lined up. Lucio took the snap and faked a handoff to Lucas, who dove over the line. The defense collapsed, and Lucio drew back and found Kenny open on the other side of the mass of bodies.

The fake worked. Kenny grabbed the ball, turned, and took off running.

A cornerback spotted the fake and gave chase, but it was too late. Kenny sprinted into the end zone for the game-winning six points and a spot in the Supreme Bowl next weekend.

Romeo ran into the end zone to celebrate, with Lucio close behind.

"See?" Kenny said. "Told you you could do this!"

* * *

Back at Bader Ginsburg Middle School, the boys showered and changed. Everyone poured out to the parking lot to go home.

Kenny, though, drifted down the hall farther, away from the exits.

"Where are you going?" Romeo asked, already with one foot out the door to the path home.

"I have some investigating to do," Kenny told his friend.

"Here?" Romeo asked. "In case you forgot, someone broke a display case at Wellstone, not here. What do you think you'll find here?"

"I was thinking about what you said," Kenny replied. "Anyone could have been wearing Jasper's jersey, and his jersey was in his locker on Friday after the game."

Romeo paused for a moment as realization dawned on his face. "So you think maybe someone other than Jasper came and got it," he said. "All right, I'm in."

"Cool," Kenny said. He turned to walk down the main hall. "First stop, main office."

# CHAPTER 9

# UNEXPECTED HELP

"Oh, I don't think that would be proper," said Harold, the office assistant. He was usually the last staff member to leave at night.

"But it's important," Kenny protested. "If we can see security video footage from outside the locker room on Sunday, we might be able to prove Jasper didn't do it."

Harold shook his head. "I just don't . . . ," he said. "Look, I don't even know how to access the darn video. So even if I wanted to show it to you, I don't know how."

"So who does?" Romeo asked.

Harold glanced at his watch. "Scott in security," he said. "His shift just started. He's down in the basement. He probably knows how. But again, it's not proper. He probably won't let you."

Kenny couldn't walk fast enough out of the office and down the school's back stairs. He found Scott at the security desk, with four CCTVs around him, each showing a grainy image of somewhere in the school.

He sat up, startled, when Kenny and Romeo walked into his office.

"What—" he said. "What are you guys doing down here?"

Scott was a young guy, probably the youngest person on staff at Bader Ginsburg.

"Harold told us to come down here to watch the security video from this past weekend," Kenny said. He leaned up next to Scott and peered at the CCTVs.

"He what?" Scott asked. "I'd better give him a call. I don't have authorization to—"

"Okay, okay," Kenny admitted. "He didn't say we *could* see the footage. But he did say we should ask you."

Scott shook his head. "Nice try," he said. "But first of all, it's a big pain in the neck to find the footage on the drives. Second, I could probably get fired. I'm only supposed to show the video to senior members of staff and, like, the police or something."

"But it's important," Kenny said. "We—"

Scott got up from his chair. "That's enough," he said. He shuffled the boys out of the office. "You're not even supposed to be down here. Now get going."

Kenny's shoulders and spirits sagged. "Fine," he said. "Thanks for nothing."

"Good night," Scott said, and he slammed the office door closed behind them.

\* \* \*

The boys walked slowly down the main hall. They stopped in front of the trophy case. A big gap was apparent in the center. That's where the Supreme Bowl would go in the years the Badgers won it.

"We barely managed to win today," Kenny said sadly. "We don't stand a chance against the Warriors with Lucio starting at QB."

"We might," Romeo said. "He pulled it off today."

"He also iced his arm the whole ride back from the game," Kenny said. "I bet he'll be too sore to practice on Monday."

Romeo shrugged.

"You shrug too much," Kenny said.

Romeo shrugged again. He squinted into the trophy case at one of the team photos.

"Hey, look at this kid," Romeo said. "Does he look familiar?"

"I doubt it," Kenny said. "That photo is from like ten years ago. Those kids are long gone. They're all done with college by now, even."

"No, I know," Romeo said. "But I swear I know this kid."

Kenny leaned in next to him to look. "Maybe," he said. "Who cares?"

"Let's see," Romeo said. "His name is . . . Scott Pearson."

"Wonderful," Kenny said, turning away from the trophy case. "Yippee for Scott Pearson. Never heard of him. Let's go. I'm hungry."

"Yeah, I'm hungry too," Romeo said. "Wanna stop for burgers on the way home?"

Kenny reached the front door and stopped with his hand on the bar. "Wait a second," he said. "Scott Pearson. I *do* know him."

"You do?" Romeo asked.

"I know why he's familiar," Kenny said. "Come on!"

He took off sprinting down the hall and the back stairs. He pounded on the security office door.

"Scott Pearson!" he said. "Open up!"

The door flew open. "Oh," Scott said. "It's you weirdos again. Didn't I tell you you're not allowed down here?"

"Yes," Kenny said. "But I didn't tell *you* we need to see that video so we can win the Supreme Bowl."

Scott's mouth dropped open. He said in a quiet, sacred voice, "The Supreme Bowl. When I was a Badger, we didn't win. Wellstone did."

"I know," Kenny said, "and they will again this year."

"Unless we can prove that Jasper didn't steal the trophy last weekend," Romeo added.

"Oh man," Scott said. "All right. Come in. But don't tell *anyone* I showed you this."

* * *

"So this is the feed from Sunday morning, outside the boys' locker room," Scott said when he got the footage cued up.

"There!" Kenny said, pointing at the monitor when a boy appeared.

"I can see it too, kid," Scott said. "Calm down."

The boy in the video had on a black hoodie and a hat just like the one Jasper usually wore, but it wasn't Jasper. He was shorter than Jasper, and he looked like he was built for speed. The boy quickly opened the locker room door and went in.

"Who was that?" Romeo asked.

"I didn't recognize him," Kenny said. "But I hardly saw his face."

"We'll get a better look when he comes out," Scott said. "We don't have cameras inside the changing areas, obviously."

"Obviously," Romeo repeated.

They sat and watched the feed. After five minutes, he still hadn't come out.

"I'll fast-forward a bit." Scott clicked a button and the timer in the corner zoomed on: five minutes, ten minutes, twenty minutes, forty minutes . . .

"What is he doing in there?" Kenny said.

"Is there a back door or something?" Romeo asked.

"There's the field exit," Scott said. "But it's supposed to be locked on weekends. I'll switch over to that feed and—"

"Wait!" Kenny said. "I saw something."

Scott rewound a little. "Ah, there he is," he said. "But that's not him. . . . That kid wasn't wearing a football jersey."

"That's Jasper!" Romeo said. "Number fourteen jersey!"

Scott nodded. "So the other guy is still in there," he said. "Because that wasn't Jasper who went in, but that was him who came out."

"Or was it?" Kenny asked.

Romeo looked at his friend questioningly. "What do you mean?"

"Whoever that is," Kenny explained, "he was in there a long time. Long enough to . . ."

Romeo's eyes went wide. "Do laundry!" he said.

"Oh, I see," Scott said. "Wait, no I don't."

"Can't explain right now," Kenny said. "We have to catch Coach Zevrin before he locks up the athletic office for the night. Can you get us the payment records for the laundry machine in the boys' locker room?"

"The laundry—" Scott started. He shook his head. "You know what, never mind. Go find the coach. I'll get the payment records . . . somehow."

# CHAPTER 10

# DIRTY LAUNDRY

"Coach Z!" Kenny shouted, sprinting up the back hallway. Up ahead, he saw the coach locking his office door.

"Boys, what are you still doing here?" the coach asked as he put his keys in his pocket. "The bus has been back for ages. The front doors will be locked soon."

"I know," Kenny said, "but it's about Jasper. We—"

"Now, I told you already," the coach said. "There is nothing I can do. And I wouldn't even if I could. The boy made a very bad choice, and now we *all* have to live with the consequences. He's going to have to carry that weight with him for a long time. I hope—"

"But, Coach," Kenny interrupted, "Jasper didn't do it, and we can prove it."

The coach crossed his arms and looked down at Kenny and Romeo with a stern smirk and narrow eyes. "Prove it?" he said. "How?"

Just then, Scott came jogging down the hall. "It's true, Coach," he called. He held up a printout. "Here's the proof!"

"Scott Pearson!" the coach said. "You're helping these two?"

"Once a Badger, always a Badger," Scott said. "Besides, I blew that pass in the semifinal game ten years ago. The least I could do is help you win the Bowl this year."

The coach frowned at Scott. "All right, what do you have?" he asked, taking the paper from Scott.

Coach Zevrin quickly looked over the printout. "Are these . . . ," he said, confused. "Are these washing machine payments?"

"Right," Scott said. He ran his finger down the line. There had been only one payment on Sunday. "There."

"Paulsen," the coach read aloud. "Who's Paulsen?"

"It must be Tye Paulsen!" Kenny said. His heart raced as the mystery seemed to unravel. "He's the starting running back at Wellstone!"

"And he's got almost a thousand rushing yards this year," Romeo said.

"Yes," the coach said, remembering, "and that's not including the postseason. Could it really be him?"

"It has to be!" Kenny said. "He snuck in here on Sunday morning, found Jasper's jersey, realized it was disgusting, and washed it."

"Then he went back to Wellstone, smashed the case, and stole the Bowl," Romeo concluded.

"I didn't even know Wellstone cards would work in our machines," Scott said.

The coach waved him off. "It's all the same company," he said. "They collect school money for everything from laundry to lunch."

"Stay on topic," Kenny said. "We have proof right here that Jasper was framed!"

"And by a star player from Wellstone!" Romeo added.

"Just so we wouldn't have our star QB for the postseason," Scott concluded.

"This does change everything, doesn't it?" said Coach Zevrin.

"The Bowl is as good as won!" Kenny exclaimed. He and Scott high-fived.

The coach folded the printout. "I'll bring this to Principal Polaski," he said. "Hopefully we'll get this all straightened out on Monday morning."

"Monday morning?" Kenny protested. "Why not right n—"

"Monday morning!" Coach Z said. "Now *go home.*"

"Okay, Coach," Kenny said. "Monday."

He and Romeo hurried away.

"And boys!" the coach called after them.

Kenny and Romeo turned around. There were the coach and Scott, smiling at them.

"Good job," Coach said.

\* \* \*

On Monday morning, Kenny left for school an hour early. He didn't even realize how fast he'd been walking until Romeo huffed up alongside him. "We hurrying today?" Romeo asked.

"I'm just excited," Kenny said. "Since you're early, I guess you are too."

"Did you tell Jasper over the weekend?" Romeo asked.

Kenny shook his head. "I almost texted him a thousand times," he said, "but I didn't want to get his hopes up, you know, in case it doesn't work out."

Romeo nodded. "Same," he said.

They reached the front doors just as Harold was unlocking them.

"Well, well, well," Harold said when he saw them. "I heard what you two did on Friday evening."

"Pretty good, huh?" Kenny said.

"You know," Harold said as he opened the door and swung it open for the boys to go inside, "when I sent you to Scott, I didn't think for a minute he'd actually help."

"Then why did you send us to him?" Kenny asked.

"To get you out of my office," Harold said, "obviously."

The boys laughed and hustled down the back hallway to Coach Zevrin's office. They practically dove through the door.

The coach laughed. "I had a feeling you two might be here early today," he said. "No surprise, the principal over at Wellstone found the Supreme Bowl in Tye Paulsen's house early this morning."

The boys high-fived.

Principal Polaski was there too, standing next to the coach's desk. "Jasper and his parents will be here soon," she said. "You boys have a seat outside."

Kenny flashed two thumbs-up, and he and Romeo sat on the bench outside. A few minutes passed before they heard Jasper's voice carrying up the hall toward them.

"What are you two doing here?" he said, his voice still sad and angry.

"You'll find out in a minute," Kenny said. "Hi, Mr. and Mrs. Kane."

"Morning, boys," Jasper's dad said. "Didn't expect to see you two here. Do you two know anything about this prank?"

"Oh, we know all about this prank, Mr. Kane," Kenny said.

Romeo gave him a fist bump.

"Come on in, Kanes!" the principal called from inside the coach's office. The Kanes went in, and the door closed behind them.

For several minutes, it was quiet. Then, like an explosion of relief and joy, came Jasper's voice: "Really?!"

The door flew open. "You guys did this?" he said.

Kenny laughed. "Yup," he replied. "We're a couple of Sherlock Holmeses."

"It was mostly this dude," Romeo said, hooking a thumb toward Kenny. "I'm just his Watson."

Jasper threw his arms around both of them. "I'm back on the team," he said. "We're about to rock that championship game."

# CHAPTER 11

# THE BIG GAME

After four more days of practice, the big game arrived. It was Friday afternoon, the day of the Supreme Bowl.

"Honest, guys," Lucio said as he pulled on his pads. "I'm not upset about it."

"I'm sure Coach Z will give you some time if we're up," Kenny said.

"That would be great," Lucio said.

"Or if Jasper's arm goes all noodle," Romeo said.

"That would be . . . not great," Lucio said.

"Not gonna happen," Jasper said. "My arm is like hot iron today: flexible and strong."

"No worries," Lucio said as he put on his jersey. "Next year, I'll be starting QB. And if you all blow the Bowl this year, I'll win it for us then."

He laughed, and the other boys tackled him.

Coach Zevrin entered the locker room. "No more horseplay, boys. We take the field in five minutes."

"Sorry, Coach!" Romeo called out.

The boys finished getting changed and lined up on the ramp to the field.

Unlike every other game of the season and postseason so far, neither team would have home-field advantage today. Instead, this Supreme Bowl was held at Central High, the high school both Wellstone and Bader Ginsburg fed into.

In fact, next year, most of the eighth-grade boys in the Supreme Bowl would be playing for the Central Sentinels junior varsity team.

"It's been a weird postseason, boys," Coach said.

The team bounced on their toes and jogged in place. They were all fired up to start the big game.

"And thanks to some good friends and Badgers teamwork," the coach went on, "we're here in the Supreme Bowl at our best."

The boys cheered and clapped.

"On the field," the coach said, "I know you're going to show the same teamwork, hard work, and smart work that Kenny and Romeo demonstrated off the field this past week. And I know we're going to bring the Bowl home the right way: by winning it."

The boys cheered and then fell quiet as the announcer's voice boomed from the loudspeakers.

"From Wellstone Middle School," the announcer said, "the Warriors!"

The crowd cheered. The boys in the tunnel clapped as well.

"Kenny," Jasper said just as the cheering outside died down. "Thanks."

"For what?" Kenny said.

"For knowing I didn't do it," Jasper said.

"Ah, you'd never do that," Kenny said. "At least not without me and Romeo!"

They both laughed and bumped fists. The announcer's voice boomed out: "And from Bader Ginsburg Middle School, the Badgers!"

The boys ran from the tunnel, cheering as they went. Kenny was sure the crowd cheered louder too.

* * *

Benny kicked off. It went out of bounds at the Warriors forty-yard line. The Badgers defense took the field.

Jasper paced behind the bench, tossing easy throws back and forth with Lucio.

Kenny and Romeo watched from the bench.

The Warriors started their drive with a dump pass to the right sideline and a gain of two yards.

"Without their star running back," Kenny said, "they're going to have a hard time on the ground."

Tye Paulsen had been suspended from school, kicked off the football team, and made to pay for the broken trophy case. He'd even had to apologize to Jasper with all the Badgers watching.

Romeo nodded. "I almost feel bad for them," he said. "We know what it's like for one teammate to ruin it for everyone else."

Jasper cleared his throat loudly. "I heard that," he said. "And I didn't even do it!"

"You know what I mean!" Romeo replied.

Kenny laughed.

The boys watched the Warriors first push. They never managed to get the first down, so they punted into the corner, leaving the Badgers to start their drive from their own five-yard line.

As they jogged onto the field, Kenny said, "This is gonna be a tough push."

"Nah, we got our QB back," Romeo said.

"That's right," Jasper said. "And you're going long right out of the gate."

In the huddle, Jasper called for a play-action. "I'll find Kenny," he said. "I wanna see some speed, too. Get at least thirty yards out and I'll hit you."

"Break!" the boys shouted together.

The offense lined up. Romeo snapped. Jasper rolled to his right, faked a handoff to Lucas, and then fell back out of the pocket to the left.

Kenny took off at a sprint, faster than his defender. At the forty, he turned. The ball came spiraling toward him. He caught it, gained another five yards, and fell to a cornerback's tackle.

He jogged back to the huddle, clapping.

"Good to have you back, Jasper," Kenny said.

Jasper put his arm around Kenny's shoulder. "Good to be back."

\* \* \*

Despite the Warriors trouble on the ground, it was a hard-fought game. Their passing was strong, and their second-string running back even managed to put up a few good runs.

With time enough for one more play, the Badgers were down by four points at the Warriors forty-yard line.

"It's down to us," Jasper said in the huddle. "And the Warriors don't know it, but that means this game is as good as ours."

"You know it," Romeo said.

"Play five," Jasper told his teammates. "Lucas, I need you to really sell this play-action. I want Kenny in the end zone wondering where the defense went. I want you to take that fake handoff and run around the outside as hard as you can, like the game depends on it. I want the Warriors to be home in their beds tonight before they realize you never even had the ball."

The huddle laughed.

"We got this," Jasper said. He put his fist into the huddle, and the other boys joined him. "Break!"

Kenny lined up at the left end of the line in the backfield. Jasper took the snap and rolled to his right.

Kenny took off from the line, hard for two steps, and then slowed down.

Jasper mimed the handoff to Lucas, and Lucas charged the line, cut hard to his right, and then swung to sprint up the sideline on the right.

The defense went for it. They converged on Lucas as he ran on.

Kenny sprinted up the field as Jasper casually rolled out of the pocket to the left. He launched a smooth and easy pass toward the end zone.

At the five-yard line, Kenny turned, found Jasper's pass, and caught it as he stepped into the end zone.

The ref blew his whistle and threw up both arms. *Touchdown!*

The whole team charged into the end zone to celebrate.

Coach Zevrin ran from the bench. Even Scott Pearson, the security guard and long-ago Badger, ran onto the field.

Kenny let the others lift him up. Another group—including Romeo—lifted Jasper. The boys high-fived in midair.

It was the best day of Kenny's life. He made the catch, they won the game, and the Supreme Bowl would be back in the Badgers trophy case!

# ABOUT THE AUTHOR

Eric Stevens has written more than one hundred chapter books for young readers. He lives with his wife and children in Minneapolis, where he and his family enjoy kayaking, cycling, and playing tennis in the city's beautiful parks.

# GLOSSARY

alibi (al-UH-bye)—an excuse for not being somewhere or doing something

bootlegs (boot-LEGZ)—in football, it's a play called to confuse the defense

burglary (burg-GLUH-ree)—to illegally enter a building in order to steal things

conversion (kuhn-VUR-shuhn)—in football, the attempt to move the ball forward

framed (FREYMD)—to make an innocent person appear guilty of a crime

rival (RYE-vuhl)—a team that tries to win more than another team

sideline (SAHYD-lahyn)—the white lines that mark the outside of a football field

suspended (suh-SPEND-ed)—not allowed to attend school for a period of time

trespassing (TRESS-pass-sing)—entering property without permission

vandalism (VAN-duhl-ihzm)—the wrecking of property

# DISCUSSION QUESTIONS

1. Jasper stopped talking to his friends after he was suspended from school for doing something he said he didn't do. Do you think the way he handled the situation was right?

2. At first, Scott wouldn't show Kenny and Romeo video footage from the day of the crime, but something changed his mind. What was it, and why do you think it made Scott want to help the boys?

3. There is a phrase, "It's not cheating if you don't get caught." What do you think this means? Is cheating ever worth it?

# WRITING PROMPTS

1. Jasper was accused of breaking into Wellstone Middle School and stealing the Supreme Bowl trophy. Write about a time that someone accused you of doing something you did not do.

2. Write an apology as if you were the person who took the trophy.

3. Kenny and Romeo compare themselves to Sherlock Holmes and Dr. Watson. Write another mystery that Kenny and Romeo solve.

# FAMOUS FOOTBALL RIVALRIES

Football rivalries have been around almost as long as the game itself. In 1869, Princeton University (then called the College of New Jersey) played Rutgers University (also in New Jersey) in the very first game of college football, though at the time it was probably more like a soccer game. The schools' football rivalry continued all the way until 1980, when their teams no longer played each other. The rivalry continues to this day in other sports, though, especially basketball.

Perhaps the most famous rivalry in all of sports is between Army and Navy. In what is the true classic football prank, Army stole Navy's goat mascot over and over through the years, beginning in the 1950s. They once even put a photo of the stolen goat in the newspaper for the whole world to see.

In 1991, Navy finally got back at Army. They stole four mascot mules right out from under Army's nose. Army was embarrassed, and perhaps that's why Navy beat them in their football game that week 24 to 3. It was the only game Navy won that season.

Here's an old one: In 1896, Auburn University students in Auburn, Alabama, greased the train tracks so the team from Georgia Tech arriving for a football game would skid right past town. The prank worked! The train slid an extra five miles down the track, and the poor players from Georgia Tech had to walk back to Auburn. They were so wiped out, Auburn easily won the big game, 45 to 0.

# SOLVE ALL THE
# SPORTS MYSTERIES!

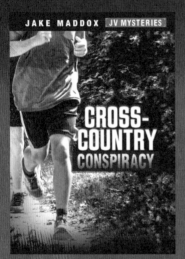

JAKE MADDOX JV MYSTERIES

**CROSS-COUNTRY**
CONSPIRACY

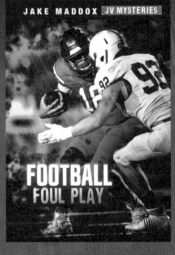

JAKE MADDOX JV MYSTERIES

**FOOTBALL**
FOUL PLAY

JAKE MADDOX JV MYSTERIES

**FULL-COURT**
MESS

JAKE MADDOX JV MYSTERIES

**GYMNASTICS**
PAYBACK